BOOK ONE

BLACKWATCH STABLES

THE SECRET OF BLACKWATCH

BLACKWATCH STABLES

The Secret of Blackwatch

Amber Cavalier Spiler

BOOKLOGIX®

BOOKLOGIX®

Alpharetta, Georgia

Copyright © 2014 by BWSS LLC

Paperback Edition November 2013

ISBN: 978-1-61005-443-0
Library of Congress Control Number: 2013920716

Cover design by Vines Media Group
www.VinesMediaGroup.com

(For information about bulk purchases, please contact the publisher.)

10 9 8 7 6 5 4 3 2   1 1 13 1 3

Printed in the United States of America

♾ This paper meets the requirements of ANSI/NISO Z39.48-1992 (Permanence of Paper)

To Bella and Lily, who inspire me every single day.

To my dad, who gave my pony wings.

To the fearless Vicki Dudasch, who knows how horses touch our souls.

The wind of heaven is that which blows
between a horse's ears.

– Arabian Proverb

CONTENTS

∪⋃∪

ACKNOWLEDGMENTS

Thanks, Mom, for encouraging my love of all things horses and allowing me to live the pony dream. Thank you, Chip, for allowing me and my girls to continue the pony dream. Thank you to my horse instructors past and present for helping me grow. Thank you to all my horsey and non-horsey girlfriends who listen to every quirky story and whole-heartedly give advice or just shake your heads in amusement. Thank you, BookLogix and Deal Pickle Creative, for reading my story.

PROLOGUE

The Book

As I sit here chewing on the end of my pen, I wonder where to start. I am slightly distracted by the sound of hooves ringing in the barn aisle. I look out the door as my youngest daughter walks her pony by my office door; she's talking to him and planning their adventures for the next day. Smiling to myself, I realize that this is what I am meant to do. I was chosen. I am the next record keeper.

"Will they believe us?" my oldest daughter asked last night when I told her my plans to share our secrets, her blue eyes staring up at me.

I don't know about everyone, but if they have ever had a pony, they will know.

I unroll the scrolls that are pages of the history of our lives. As they scatter over the old wooden desk, I know it's time to share our stories…

CHAPTER ONE

Maggie and the Barn

H er pony galloped full speed toward the darkness, white mane whipping in her face as she bent closer and whispered words of encouragement. Suddenly they were in the air, flying straight toward danger. She couldn't see the source of the danger, but she knew it was there. She could feel it. Even smell it. She reached for the weapon at her side. Weapon? She had never even held a knife before, but her hand automatically knew what to do. It was a sword of sorts. No, maybe not a sword, it was like the *skinny swords she'd seen people use in fencing. A foil. How did she know that? The rain was pouring down on them, making it hard to see the way, but she trusted her pony. There it was! Out of nowhere! She struck out at it but couldn't quite see it. The next thing she knew, she was tumbling through the air, falling again.*

∪◡∪

She awoke with a start, and she was safe and sound in her own house. Well, *safe*, but not quite sound. She had dozed off again in the attic while looking at old photo albums. This seemed to be a recent afternoon trend.

Maggie Thompson was almost twelve. She had sandy blonde hair, and she was a bit skinny and short with blue eyes. She was living in New Hampshire with her father, Jeff. Today was the one-year anniversary of her mother's death. Her dad was a financial advisor who, quite frankly, was not very outdoorsy, but her mom was... Sarah Thompson was special. She was not too tall or too short; she was slim but always seemed radiant and healthy. Sarah never sat still and could almost always be found outside. It was hard for Maggie to imagine her mom still, not dancing through the fields, humming silly tunes that no one else knew, or simply walking through the woods, chatting with the birds that always seemed to appear when she was around.

Maggie tossed the old photo album into the pile with the rest. It was no use staring at them anymore. Her mom was not coming back. No more stories of beautiful silver ponies, of girls and horses spending hours together, giggling and galloping through their young weekends. No more promises of ponies to come.

Maggie wiped the dust from her hands onto her jeans and slowly made her way down the attic stairs.

Her dad was in the big, old-fashioned kitchen; a fire was burning in the fireplace, and the smell of omelets filled the room. Omelets. That was her dad's specialty. In fact, it was one of the only things her dad could actually make on the stove.

"Maggie, do you want bacon?" her dad asked. "Oh, and go wash up, your hands are filthy! Have you been sulking in the attic again? Tomorrow morning we're taking a special trip, one that your mom always wanted you to take. Do you think that you can stop moping long enough to spend the day with me? Come on, kiddo, I know we can have some fun if we just try."

"Sure, Dad," Maggie said, trying her hardest to sound cheerful. "Just as long as I don't have to take another tour of the bank and learn how to deposit checks…again."

Jeff messed up her hair, and they continued their tradition of omelet dinner on the kitchen table.

Maggie sat in the car, looking out the window at the big snowy fields and miles of fence. She had no idea where her dad was taking her, but it almost made her giggle to see him dressed in jeans and perfectly pristine hiking boots. Hiking? Not her dad. Although he *had* been willing to try new things since her mom died. She had to give him credit for that. She looked up as the car slowed, and they turned onto a small gravel road. She looked around at all the white fence and blinked and turned to look at her dad. "Dad?"

Ahead was a large sign with a coat of arms on a painted plaid background. In big letters she read *Blackwatch Stables*. For some reason her stomach suddenly felt like she had a million butterflies flying around inside. As they crested the hill, she saw a huge dark green barn. It was perfect! A castle could not have surprised her more...or made her happier. "Dad, what is this?" Maggie whispered.

"Well, your mom always wanted you to ride. So...well, here we are. Everywhere I turned I heard Blackwatch Stables on everyone's lips, so I figured it was a sign."

As they pulled up to the barn, she thought she caught a glimpse of a dark-haired girl running. As they got out of the car, a woman came walking out. Well, it wasn't actually walking... maybe prancing wasn't quite the word either. Marching. She marched out of the barn. Cinnamon brown hair pulled back into a low ponytail, tan riding pants, tall black boots, and a plaid turtleneck shirt almost completely covered by a black wool coat. Maggie stood, not sure if she should smile or curtsy.

She held out a gloved hand and said, "Welcome, Maggie. We are quite pleased to have you here. My name is Ms. Cavalieri. Welcome to Blackwatch Stables." She then looked over at Maggie's dad, shook his hand too, and murmured, "Welcome, Jeff." Looking back at Maggie briefly, she lifted an eyebrow and turned on her heel. "Follow me."

Maggie could not believe her eyes when she walked into the barn. It was spotless. Brass nameplates on each door and plaid trunks lined the aisles. Each stall door had a black *x* with a horseshoe twisted out to hold the leather halters. The halters had brass nameplates as well. Every horse had a plaid blanket, and they all turned curiously as she walked through the barn.

Halfway down the barn, they came to a stop in front of an empty stall. "This stall is for your pony, Maggie."

Maggie yelped, "What?!"

"Ms. Cavalieri has promised me that she will be able to find you the perfect pony," said Jeff. "I think this will help cheer you up and make you feel close to your mother again." Jeff took a deep breath. "We don't want to waste all those pony camps we sent you to, do we?"

Maggie's mouth popped open.

"I have directions to a local horse sale going on tonight. I feel quite certain that you will find Maggie's pony there."

"Uh, tonight? Well, that seems a bit sudden. Are you sure?" Jeff asked, and Maggie just stood there, looking back and forth between her bewildered father and the firm Ms. Cavalieri.

"Yes," Ms. Cavalieri said. "Maggie, you will pick your pony tonight, and tomorrow, when you arrive, your pony will be waiting for you right here in this stall. Now, go find Katie. She will send you home with some riding breeches and boots. Please wear a Blackwatch Stables shirt and come dressed and ready to start your new adventure."

Maggie walked through the barn, peeking into the stalls as she walked. Right next to her stall there was a black pony munching happily on her hay. She was about fourteen hands and solid black, not a bit of white on her. She had a long, thick mane and tail. *I'll never have a pony this cute,* thought Maggie as she admired the pony.

"Hi!"

Maggie jumped; she hadn't heard anyone walk up behind her. A girl with long dark brown hair braided into two neat braids was standing there smiling at her.

"I didn't mean to startle you. I see you've met Lily. Isn't she darling? I was so happy when I found her! Bet you're going to find a fantastic pony too! Oh, I'm sorry—I'm Katie." The girl stuck out her hand, and Maggie reached out and shook it.

"Hi, Katie. I think I was supposed to find you and get some stuff from you," said Maggie.

"Yep, I have it all ready. Ms. Cavalieri is very specific. Tan riding breeches, clean tall boots, and a Blackwatch shirt and jacket. Oh, and always remember to braid your hair. She hates sloppiness, and hair hanging out of your helmet is sloppy. Wait until you see how often we clean our tack! Not to mention our ponies." Katie smiled and put her arm around Maggie's shoulders. "Don't look worried; it's hard work, but it's totally worth it!" Katie then gave Maggie a big hug and said, "Welcome home." Then she turned and skipped away, dark braids bouncing down her back.

CHAPTER TWO

Pony Sale

Maggie looked at the directions again. Surely Ms. Cavalieri had made a mistake. There was no way this broken-down farm could be where Ms. Cavalieri thought she would find the perfect pony.

"Come on, Maggie, let's find your pony," said Dad. "I can't imagine that we will find anything here, but we'll give it a shot."

Maggie hopped out of the car and was so nervous that she almost grabbed her dad's hand. As they walked up the muddy drive, they could hear the sounds of the auctioneer. They walked into the run-down barn and saw ponies and horses in one big pen together. Some were nervously pacing and wondering what was going to happen to them, while others stood with heads down, not expecting anything good. The sight of all these sad, dirty ponies and horses almost made Maggie cry. As she stood looking around, a tall, handsome, dark-haired man approached them.

"Looking for a pony for the little girl?" He smiled, but the smile did not reach his eyes.

As he looked at her slyly, Maggie realized he became less handsome and more evil-looking.

He looked at Maggie suspiciously, as if he knew her and had seen her doing something very naughty. "And your name, young lady?" He looked right in her eyes.

"Uh...Maggie. Maggie Thompson." Maggie stuttered a bit.

"I'm Stephen. For a minute I thought you were someone else. Never mind, go ahead and step into that pen. Let's see if we can find you the pony of your dreams."

Jeff looked at Maggie apprehensively. "Go ahead, honey."

So Maggie climbed through the warped fence and started walking around the horses: paints, grays, bays, and chestnuts. All dirty, all sad. It almost broke Maggie's heart just standing with them. Then she spotted a bay mare, different from the others. She was quite cute! She looked utterly out of place in this barn of misfits. As Maggie started walking toward the pony, eyes glued on her, she barely noticed a dirty gray pony walking her way. She barely noticed until the pony stepped right in her path and stopped. Maggie practically bumped into the pony before she noticed her.

"Move, pony," Maggie said impatiently. "Move!" But the pony stood her ground. "Come on, pony, get out of the way." But the pony looked right at her and wouldn't budge. Maggie sighed and started to walk around the pony. The pony snorted and backed up, blocking Maggie's way. Maggie couldn't help laughing at the tenacity of the pony. She felt like the dirty gray pony knew exactly why she was there. She scratched the pony on the face and smiled. "Well, you do have a pretty little face—too bad about the rest of you. Now move out of my way so I can go see that lovely bay pony." The gray pony snorted again and shook her head. She wasn't moving. She turned and looked Maggie right in the eyes, then pushed Maggie to the ground.

Stephen came rushing over. "Are you okay?" He slapped the pony's neck. "Get out of the way, you old nag!" he yelled. "You are going to be dog food tomorrow!"

Maggie's dad was by her side. "Surely you're kidding?" asked Jeff.

"Nope, this pony is no use to us. Now, let's go look at that bay!"

Maggie stood, shocked by the thought of the gray pony becoming dog food. "No!" Maggie said, quietly at first. "NO! I want this pony!"

Both Jeff and Stephen looked at her like she was crazy. "What?" they asked in unison.

"I want this pony!" said Maggie again. The gray pony had been staring at her like she was crazy too. Then she pushed her face into Maggie's chest.

"Forget it," said Stephen, "this pony has already been sold to the slaughterhouse." Stephen nodded his head toward the large man across the paddock.

Maggie wrapped her arms around the pony's face and whispered, "I will save you. I won't let you go."

Jeff grabbed Maggie's arm, looked at Stephen, and said, "We'll see about that!" Quickly her dad walked directly up to the man Stephen had nodded to, and—before Maggie knew what happened—they exchanged money and shook hands. "Well, Maggie, go say good-night to your pony. She will be delivered to Blackwatch Stables first thing in the morning."

Maggie couldn't believe her ears—this dirty, fuzzy, gray nag was all hers!

Maggie was up before the sun the next morning. She couldn't have slept more than a few hours, but she was wide awake. She had spent the first half of the night trying to decide on a name. *Stormy.* That was what she had decided to name the gray, shaggy pony. Maggie thought the name was just okay, but that was the best she could come up with so far.

As she ran down the stairs, she could already hear her dad moving around in the kitchen. "Morning, Sunshine," he said, "something special for you on this special morning?"

"Dad, you made pancakes?" Maggie grinned. "This is very special!" She hopped up on a stool and pulled her plate closer to her. Her dad slid her a glass of OJ, and she sat thoughtfully chewing her breakfast. "So, how about Stormy?" Maggie asked her dad.

"Nope," he replied, "looks like it will be cold but sunny." He winked at her.

"Dad! I mean for a name for the pony."

He was quiet for a moment. "What about your mom's pony's name? Chloe?"

Maggie looked up at her dad. "I thought about that too, but it doesn't fit my pony."

"Well, honey, it's your pony. You name her whatever you want."

Maggie finished her pancakes in record time and raced back up the stairs to put on her riding clothes. She stood in front of the mirror, braiding her hair just the way Katie taught her. She could hear Katie's words of advice in her mind, *Make sure that you don't have any strands of hair hanging out of your helmet, shirttails tucked in, belt on, and always zip your jacket!* As Maggie stood looking at herself in the mirror, she liked what she saw. She knew this was what she was meant to do. Only she pictured doing it on a cuter pony. Oh well, hopefully once she cleaned up the pony, she would look better too.

CHAPTER THREE

Meet Bella

B ye, Dad!" Maggie waved as her dad pulled away from Blackwatch Stables. *Okay*, she thought, *here we go!*

As soon as she walked through the door, she was greeted by Katie, who was practically jumping up and down with excitement. "I knew you'd find the perfect pony!" she cried. "She is lovely, and she is already getting along with

Lily! Bella and Lily are acting like they're long-lost friends!"

Maggie looked at Katie sideways. "Who's Bella?"

Well, that sent Katie into a fit of giggles. "Come with me, silly. I'll show you your stuff while the ponies finish breakfast."

They walked into the tack room, and Katie switched on the light. Maggie looked around at the racks and racks of saddles and bridles. She closed her eyes and breathed in the warm smell of leather. It made her feel safe. It felt like she was home.

"Maggie?" Katie grabbed her arm. "Maggie, come over here and let me show you your tack. We figured that a size 16 saddle would fit you best, and we already have a pony bridle cleaned and ready to go. We all use Blackwatch plaid saddle pads, and they are on the rack in the back of the tack room. Make sure you put your pad neatly back when you are finished or Ms. Cavalieri will have a cow."

Maggie looked around in awe. She had never imagined that she would have a saddle to use. She thought that she would find a used one online. "How did I get a saddle?" asked Maggie.

"I don't know." Katie shrugged. "But it's yours. Look." On the cantle of the saddle was a shiny brass nameplate that read *Maggie Thompson* in black print. This was unbelievable!

Just then, another girl walked into the tack room. She was a bit taller than Maggie and Katie with long brown braids and a few freckles across her nose and cheeks. "Hi, Sam. This is Maggie. She's finally here!" said Katie.

"Well, make sure she knows the rules! Oh, and show her where all her grooming stuff is in her trunk. Maggie, I check all the trunks once a month, so make sure that you keep it in order. I also check your tack to make sure you're taking proper care of it. Ms. Cavalieri will check your pony daily. Oh, by the way, your pony is lovely. And, Maggie, welcome home!" Sam smiled and walked back out of the tack room, arms loaded with saddle, bridle, and saddle pads.

Maggie looked wide-eyed at Katie. "What was that?"

Katie laughed. "That's Sam. She's the oldest— barely—and she's the captain of the barn. Don't let her worry you. She's to the point, but she is very kind. If you ever need help with your pony, she will take care of her as if she were her own. The ponies love her too. Okay, follow me!"

Katie led Maggie down the barn to a stall that had a nameplate on it that read *Bella Tempesta* and then below it read *(Bella)*. Maggie wondered, *Who is this Bella pony?*

In front of the stall was a beautiful, shiny, dark blue trunk with painted plaid on the lid. "The plaid is called Blackwatch. Get it? Blackwatch? Go ahead and look inside."

Maggie unhooked the brass latches and gasped when she opened the trunk. Brushes, curry combs, hoof picks, folded rags, hoof oil, ointment, and bandages…anything she would ever need was in this trunk.

"Holy cow!" exclaimed Maggie, "How in the world…?"

Katie shrugged. "Ms. Cavalieri is very serious about horse care. We have all the tools, and it's our job to use them."

Just then Ms. Cavalieri came marching down the aisle. "I see you're dressed properly, and it appears that Katie has shown you around. Have you greeted your pony yet? You made a superb choice, by the way."

Maggie looked at Ms. Cavalieri with a combination of respect and confusion. She was sure that this pony would be the laughingstock of the barn. "Well, there was this bay…" Maggie started to explain.

"Nonsense. Your pony doesn't make mistakes. You are hers. She is yours. Perfect match. Well, go ahead and get her out. Show her to us."

Maggie looked up, startled to see girls coming out of the stalls and curiously making their way toward her. Ms. Cavalieri opened the stall door with the *Bella* nameplate. "Oh!" This made perfect sense now; they were all looking at the wrong pony, and so she said, "My pony's name is Stormy, Ms. Cavalieri."

With an arched eyebrow, Ms. Cavalieri looked over her shoulder and said, "Your pony doesn't like to be called *Stormy*, she likes to go by *Bella*. Her full name is *Bella Tempesta*, which means *beautiful storm*, but *Bella* is fine with her."

What? Okay, Maggie was convinced that Ms. Cavalieri was more than a little wacky. So her pony "likes to go by Bella," but how did they even know what Maggie had named her? As she looked around at all the other girls, she noticed that none of them looked surprised. *Great, a whole barn full of crazies.* Ms. Cavalieri appeared from the stall with Maggie's shaggy, gray pony that was all decked out in a navy halter and guess what else? A Blackwatch blanket. All the girls *oohed* and *aahed* at the pony. Maggie took the lead rope and scratched the pony on her forehead. The pony started rubbing against Maggie.

"Well, Bella, I guess we are a family now." As she said this, Bella nickered, and Maggie could swear she heard the words, "Welcome home."

ᘮᘭᘮᘭ

"Come on, Maggie, this way." Maggie led Bella through the barn. Katie had helped her take off Bella's blanket, reminding her to hang it neatly on the bar outside her stall. Now they were making their way toward the wash rack. It was sparkling clean, as wash racks go, equipped with heat lamps and hot water.

"Winter is no excuse for a dirty pony," Ms. Cavalieri had reminded them. There were shelves with buckets, sponges, shampoos, and conditioners. Katie was already warming up the water and filling a bucket with soapy bubbles.

"First clean her feet," said Katie. "This will also ensure that you run your hands down her legs to check for injuries. Here, I'll show you." Together the girls washed and soaped and scrubbed and combed the pony. Bella had one hind leg cocked, and her eyes were half closed. Maggie was sure that Bella was completely enjoying this "pony spa" experience. After they scraped all the water off of Bella, they went to work on her mane and tail. Katie sprayed something on Bella's tail that made it soft, and it wasn't long before all the tangles were gone.

"You shouldn't comb it every day, but I would wash, condition, and spray it a few times a week. Now let's pull her mane," said Katie. "We have a special pulling comb with a razor in it. This makes mane pulling a little easier. Oh, and the ponies like it better too." Standing on buckets, the girls took turns combing and pulling Bella's mane until it was all one length and uniform.

"I have a feeling that Bella loves her long forelock," said Maggie thoughtfully. "Let's just leave it long."

Katie agreed, and they stepped back to admire their work. "She's beautiful!" exclaimed Katie.

Maggie stood back and looked at the pony. She did look a lot better, but beautiful might be an exaggeration. Bella snorted and looked at Maggie, and then she snorted and pushed Maggie down right onto the wet cement with her head, as if to say, "Silly girl, I am beautiful."

CHAPTER FOUR

First Lesson

Katie came running out to greet Maggie. "Today's the day! I can't wait to see Bella under saddle! I bet she's wonderful! Come on, I'll help you tack up."

Maggie pushed the stall door open, and Bella nickered a warm greeting. "Good morning, Bella," said Maggie as she picked shavings out of her forelock. "You look rested." The pony nodded as if she understood. "I got some rest as well. I dreamt of riding you and hope you're as good in real life as you were in my dreams." Maggie grabbed the halter and slipped it over Bella's head. She led her out of the stall to the crossties.

Katie was so excited that she was practically bouncing. "I have your saddle, pad, and bridle out already. I'll help you brush her."

As the girls brushed the pony, chatting and giggling, Sam walked by, leading her still-steaming pony, Jazz. "Make sure you pick her hooves and check her legs! I'm going to finish cooling down Jazz, and then I'll watch your lesson."

Maggie's stomach jumped a little at the thought of others watching. It had been months since her last riding lesson and that was at a little camp, not a big fancy stable.

She took the reins and started leading Bella through the barn and out toward the riding ring. With every step, the knot in her stomach tightened. *What if Bella bucks? What if she can't be ridden? What if I fall off in front of everyone?* As she stepped into the sunlight, her worries started to ease. They walked into the ring, and Katie shut the gate behind her. Sam came marching over and checked her saddle and bridle.

"Looks good, Maggie. You'll be just fine." Sam held Bella while Maggie climbed up the mounting block and onto her pony for the very first time.

Ms. Cavalieri, who was leaning up against the rail, said, "How does it feel, Maggie? To be exactly where you belong?"

Maggie gathered her reins, and as she looked toward Ms. Cavalieri, she realized that almost all the kids from the barn were gathered around watching. There was another pony in the ring cooling down from his lesson, and it seemed like the cute roan pony was watching too.

"Janie, make sure Tiger is cool before you leave," said Ms. Cavalieri.

"Yes, ma'am," replied Janie.

"Okay, Maggie, let's walk," said Ms. Cavalieri, all of her attention now on Maggie and Bella.

Maggie squeezed her legs and murmured, "Walk, Bella." And to her surprise, Bella moved into a lovely marching walk, ears pricked and happy to start.

"So, Maggie, what's the first thing we do when we get on a new pony?" asked Ms. Cavalieri.

Maggie shrugged, feeling silly in front of her new friends. Then, in her head she heard, *Check my whoa.*

Huh? "Whoa?" Maggie said in surprise. Bella stopped.

"Yes! Very good, Maggie. We always check our brakes first. Walk on," said Ms. Cavalieri.

Bella started walking before Maggie had the chance to do anything. Maggie slipped a hand off the reins to give Bella a pat on the neck.

"Okay, let's pick up a posting trot," said Ms. Cavalieri.

"Trot, Bella," said Maggie, and her pony immediately swung into a trot.

"Very nice. Shoulders back, chin up. Ride like a princess. Trust your pony, Maggie. She wants to take care of you," Ms. Cavalieri said as she stood with perfect posture in the middle of the ring.

Before long, Maggie and Bella were cantering around the ring like they were made for each other. Ms. Cavalieri was constantly telling her to keep her hands quiet or to push her heels down, but all in all, it was a fantastic first ride.

"Okay, walk her around. She hasn't been worked like this in years, so make sure she's nice and cool. Good job today, ladies." Ms. Cavalieri turned and walked to the rail.

As Maggie patted Bella and walked around, she noticed the other girls smiling encouragingly at her. This was definitely where she belonged!

CHAPTER FIVE

Over the Hills

Maggie was up before her alarm went off. It was Saturday! Finally! She quickly brushed her hair and teeth and raced down the stairs toward the kitchen. She could hear her dad shuffling around already. "Morning, Maggie, what's the plan today?"

Maggie sat at the counter and pulled her plate of eggs toward her while her dad poured her some OJ. "Well, today a few of us are going to hack the ponies around the farm!"

Her dad looked at her for a moment. "Okay, I have no idea what you just said."

Maggie rolled her eyes. "We are going out over the hills and through the woods." She giggled.

"Well, you girls be careful and stick together!" Her dad laughed and poured himself a cup of coffee.

"We will, Dad," said Maggie, smiling.

Jeff looked at Maggie over his steaming cup of coffee. He couldn't believe how much she had changed in the last couple of months. Losing Sarah had been hard on them, but Maggie seemed to be doing much better since Bella had come into their lives. She seemed to be Maggie's magic pill.

As Maggie finished her breakfast, she took her stuff to the sink to wash the dishes. "Leave it, Maggie. I'll do it. Finish getting ready and I'll 'hack' you over to that pony of yours."

"Thanks, Dad," Maggie said and walked over to give him a hug. "Thanks for everything."

The barn was busy this crisp morning. All the girls and ponies were super excited. It had been a while since they had been out of the ring, and it was sure to be tons of fun. Sam was busy tacking up Jazz while running around to check all the other girls and ponies. Janie was giggling and telling the girls that she was going to be the first one to make it to the bridge. Tiger snorted and nodded his head in agreement, and all the girls laughed.

There was Reece, who Maggie didn't know very well yet, on her pony, Athena, and Reece's best friend Lyndsey on her bay pony, Shooter. There were a few other girls as well who Maggie was still getting to know.

Katie was finished tacking Lily, and both of them were waiting impatiently on Maggie and Bella. Bella practically pushed her head into the bridle. "Chill out, Bella, I'm going as fast as I can." Bella nickered and rubbed her gray head on Maggie.

Ms. Cavalieri came marching through the girls and ponies, checking girths and occasionally wiping boots. "We should always, always look our best, even when going on a casual hack. It's our uniform, and it keeps us safe." Once everyone passed inspection, they all started taking turns on the mounting block, except Sam, who managed to get on all by herself. Ms. Cavalieri mounted her golden palomino, Willow, and everyone was ready to go.

The girls laughed as they rode their ponies through the woods. Patches of sunlight shone through the trees, making an ordinary day seem magical. The ponies trotted along, enjoying the day every bit as much as their girls. "Ready?" asked Janie as she pulled Tiger up and faced them. "Let's race to the bridge!" All the girls laughed.

"Janie and Sam think everything is a competition," laughed Katie.

Ms. Cavalieri pulled up and smiled. "On your marks, get set...go!" But before Ms. Cavalieri could even say "go," Sam and Jazz were off and running. Janie seemed to know this would happen, because she was right on Jazz's tail.

"Come on, Maggie!" shouted Katie.

Maggie glanced up at Ms. Cavalieri who winked and said, "Don't want to come in last, do you?"

Maggie tentatively asked Bella to canter, and Bella willingly followed the other ponies. "Wow! This is fun, Bella!" shouted Maggie into Bella's ear. Bella squealed and cantered faster, passing Lyndsey and Shooter as well as Reece and Athena. She galloped up alongside Katie and Lily and decided that this was a great place to be.

Katie looked over at Maggie and yelled, "There's a log up ahead. Don't worry, Bella will jump it! Just wrap your pinky around her mane, get in two-point position, and hang on! This will be fun!"

Fun? What? Maggie almost pulled up. But she heard a voice in her head. *Don't worry. You can do this. You were born to do this.* So Maggie, half convinced she was going crazy, wrapped her fingers into Bella's mane and got up into two-point. Holding her breath, she saw the log up ahead.

"Breathe, Maggie, you're fine." Ms. Cavalieri was right beside her.

The log was approaching at a rapid speed; Maggie felt Bella gather her body, and then the next thing she knew, they were on the other side. Bella squealed again and bucked in celebration.

"Wow, Bella! That was fun!" Ahead Maggie saw the other ponies slowing, and she realized she had reached the bridge.

Sam was laughing. "Come on, Janie, you know Jazz can fly like the wind. Tiger is younger; he'll catch on soon."

"Don't let her fool you," whispered Katie. "Sam will try her hardest to never let anyone beat Jazz. Jazz feels the same and taunts the other ponies relentlessly. These ponies are made for their humans."

As the girls walked their steaming ponies over the bridge, Maggie was enthralled with the beautiful green meadow before her. *This is like a fairy tale.* She almost expected a troll and some billy goats to hop out of the stream. Bella snorted and shook her head as if she could read Maggie's thoughts and was agreeing.

"Hop down, girls, and let your ponies drink some water," said Ms. Cavalieri. "Loosen your girths a bit and let them relax."

The girls did as they were told and soon were all laughing and comparing rides. Before long, Ms. Cavalieri told them that it was time to start heading back. As Maggie tightened her girth, she noticed that the sky was getting dark. Bella seemed to notice too and was starting to shift around like she was in a hurry. "Okay, girl, I'm going as fast as I can," Maggie said soothingly as she stepped from a log into her stirrup. All the ponies were dancing around like they were eager to go.

"Ladies," said Ms. Cavalieri, "pick your partner and don't separate no matter what! Your ponies will make sure you get home safely so just hang on and trust your mount."

Katie and Maggie looked at each other, and Lily and Bella touched noses. "Partner," giggled Katie nervously, "I'll lead. Don't worry, this will be an adventure!"

As she said this, the wind started to whip, and Ms. Cavalieri began leading the girls and ponies across the bridge. Once they crossed, they picked up a brisk trot and headed toward the farm. Maggie kept talking to Bella as she tried to keep herself calm. She just tried to focus on Lily's thick black tail as they trotted through the windy path in the woods.

Maggie was startled by a loud clap of thunder, and in the next stride, all the ponies were cantering. Before she could even worry about it, the log was in her path, and they were over it in a second. She could hear Willow cantering behind her, but Willow seemed to be falling behind.

As she glanced over her shoulder, Ms. Cavalieri yelled, "I'm going to make sure nothing is following us."

Following us? Maggie thought. *Who in the world could be following us?* But she kept going.

Suddenly she heard a crash, and she pulled up and turned around. A giant tree had fallen across the path! Then she noticed Ms. Cavalieri galloping down the path right in the direction of the tree! There was no way she could stop and no way she could clear that tree! The next thing Maggie knew, Willow was in the air and landing at her side.

"Ride, Maggie," said Ms. Cavalieri, "and close your mouth."

Maggie turned Bella, and they continued their canter back toward the farm.

"Girls, cool those ponies out well. I don't want a barn of sick ponies because you were all careless. When your ponies are dry, blanket them and make sure they have plenty of hay and water."

Maggie had thrown a cooler over Bella and was hand walking her when she stopped Katie and asked, "Did you see Ms. Cavalieri jump that tree? Katie, that wasn't a little log! That was a tree! Branches and all! There is no way she should have been able to jump that!" Maggie was confused— she knew that jump was impossible.

Katie winked at Maggie and said, "Come on, Maggie, it's not like she grew wings and flew over it. Willow is just an amazing jumper. She can practically fly."

Maggie shot a dirty look in Katie's direction. She knew Katie was teasing her, but she knew what she saw. "Bella, you saw it too. You know I'm not crazy."

Bella snorted and rubbed up against her as if to say, "Yes, Maggie, you saw it, and I did too."

Minutes later, Maggie's thoughts were interrupted by Sam, who was checking to make sure all the ponies were cooled properly. As Maggie checked Bella's water and hay and hugged her good-bye, she wondered what type of adventures she had to look forward to in the future.

Maggie hugged Katie as they made plans for their next riding adventure. "I'll see you tomorrow," said Katie as she ran out of the barn.

Maggie waved and wondered what was keeping her dad. As she sat on her trunk, watching Bella munch contentedly on her hay, she heard voices coming from the office. Maggie started walking toward the office to ask if Ms. Cavalieri had heard from her dad.

As she approached, she heard Reece say, "Are you sure Bella is the one?"

"Positive," replied Ms. Cavalieri, "Bella looks exactly like Chloe. She's got that beautiful dished face, very delicate long legs, and if you look closely, you will see that the marking on her face is shaped like a heart. It's hard to see on a gray horse, but it's there."

"So when do you think it will happen?" asked Reece.

"It will happen soon. When horse and rider trust each other, the magic will start happening."

Maggie tiptoed away from the office and ran quietly back to Bella's stall. Her hand shook as she opened the stall door and pushed Bella's forelock to the side. *She really does have a pretty face,* thought Maggie. *How did I never notice that before?* She could barely tell there was a marking on her forehead. She reached in the water bucket and wet her hand. She rubbed it on the pony's face. Carefully she traced the pink skin. *A heart!*

A perfect heart! Could it be that Maggie found a pony at a dumpy horse sale that was the daughter of her mother's horse? What kind of magic was this?

CHAPTER SIX

Custom-Made Ponies

Maggie and Katie were hacking their ponies bareback in the back field. As usual, they were laughing and having the best time ever. Even the ponies seemed to be in great spirits. "Katie," Maggie said, "how did you get Lily?"

"Well," said Katie thoughtfully, "I started taking lessons here shortly after my father died. After about a year or so, Lily just kind of showed up. Ms. Cavalieri had a conversation with my mother and just like that," Katie snapped her fingers, "she was mine!" Katie leaned down and hugged Lily. When she did, Lily nickered quietly. "I feel like we were meant for each other, like she was always mine." Katie rubbed her pony. "Did you know that my dad used to ride? He had a Friesian named Dance."

Maggie looked at Katie and said, "A Friesian? Don't you think it's weird that Lily looks like a tiny Friesian?"

Katie shrugged. "I never really thought about it."

Maggie looked at Katie and whispered, "I think that Bella is the daughter of my mom's horse, Chloe. I overheard Ms. Cavalieri say something about it."

Katie sighed. "Yes, you're right. Maggie, most of our horses here are descendants of our parents' horses. I know it's weird, but we are all a part of some crazy horse and rider line that has been around forever." Katie smiled at Maggie's stunned expression. "Haven't you ever wondered why you love horses so much? Why riding is so natural to you? Didn't you wonder why Bella insisted that you take her home? Maggie, you are literally riding a horse that was made for you."

Maggie just sat there on her "custom-made" pony with her mouth open.

"She's okay, Bella," giggled Katie. Bella snorted and shook her head. When Maggie continued to sit there, Bella turned around and nipped her leg.

Maggie blinked and rubbed her pony. *I sure have lots of things to sort out in my head.* Bella nodded in agreement.

As Maggie walked into the barn, she noticed all the girls were gathered around the bulletin board. "Ms. Cavalieri is calling a meeting, and if you plan on showing this season you'd better show up!" said Sam. "And I know you plan on showing this season, right?" It was more of a statement than a question.

Showing? Maggie thought. It had never really crossed her mind. *We have made so much progress in the past couple of months, but will my little horse sale pony ever be good enough to show?*

"Good day, ladies." Ms. Cavalieri walked around the corner. "I have a list of the shows Blackwatch Stables will be attending this year. There are different organizations and circuits you can try, and some of you may do them all. So just take these home and discuss it with your parents and let me know what you are willing to commit to this season." Ms. Cavalieri started passing them out. "Sam and Lyndsey, your Eventing information is on the second page. Katie, we have a couple of Combined Training shows for you to try this year. The rest of you will be expected to do at least one Combined Training show this year. Janie, don't groan, I can see your face. Dressage is the basis of everything, and if you can't get through a basic

Dressage class, you shouldn't be jumping. Maggie, talk to me later this week, and we can discuss your goals. At Blackwatch Stables we do Hunter/Jumper shows or Eventing, so we can decide together what best suits you and your pony. However, I don't let my kids show Cross Country until the age of twelve. No exceptions." Katie made a face, and Ms. Cavalieri saw it and gave her "the look."

All of the girls stood around together, looking over the schedule and planning their horse show year.

"Well, Maggie, what do you think you will want to do?" asked Katie.

Maggie shrugged. "I don't even know the difference."

"In Eventing you get to do three phases," said Sam, "Dressage, Cross Country, and Stadium Jumping. It's the most fun!"

Janie rolled her eyes. "In Hunter/Jumpers it's not just about getting over the jump, but you have to do it with style and precision. With class. Besides…Dressage is B-O-R-I-N-G."

Sam stepped up again. "Dressage is the necessary evil that gets you to Cross Country, and Cross Country R-O-C-K-S! Who needs 'style'? Totally overrated."

Maggie was totally confused.

Lyndsey—who was usually very shy—stepped forward and said, "Dressage isn't boring; it's lovely. It's like ballet. It requires concentration, strength, and a great partnership between horse and rider. No matter what you choose, Dressage will only make you a better rider."

Katie laughed at Maggie's face. "Come on, Maggie, let's tack up! We have a lesson in thirty minutes and only time will tell."

"Chin up, Maggie! Outside rein! Let go of that inside rein and trust your pony! Leg! Leg! Good!"

Maggie was out of breath, and her mind was boggled, but she did exactly what Ms. Cavalieri told her. She would do anything to become a better rider.

"Shoulders back! Now sit! Nice! Maggie, did you feel that?"

Maggie grinned and gave Bella a big hug. *What a great jump.* Now if only she could do it over a whole course.

"Maggie, you are doing much better. Don't worry right now about whether you want to be an Eventer or a Hunter/Jumper. Let your pony decide. No matter which you do, you have to learn proper equitation, and your pony has to learn proper form. With that, you can do anything. Now cool her out, wash her, and tell her how wonderful she's doing. Don't forget to thank her." Ms. Cavalieri had a great way of ending each lesson on a good note.

Ms. Cavalieri started working with Katie and Lily, and Maggie continued walking Bella until she was cool. She hopped down and pushed her stirrups up. Bella gently rubbed her face against Maggie.

"You were good today, Bella, thank you." Bella snorted and rubbed Maggie again.

Maggie was finishing up with Bella when Katie came in leading Lily.

"Hey, Maggie, want to see if you can stay the night tonight? I already asked my mom, and she said it is fine with her. We're ordering pizza."

Maggie smiled. "I'd love that! I'll ask Dad when he comes to pick me up."

Maggie hadn't had a sleepover since her mom had died. In fact, she had barely spoken to all her old friends since then. It seemed like they just didn't want to talk to her anymore. Or maybe she was the one who wasn't talking to them? Either way, it would be great to have some girl time with someone who understood horses.

Maggie put Bella away and helped Katie bathe Lily. Together they spoke to Maggie's dad and reassured him that Katie's mom was indeed in on the plan. As Jeff and Maggie drove home together, he quizzed her on her time at the barn until he was satisfied that Maggie had thoroughly enjoyed herself.

∪◡∪

"You ready, kiddo?" Jeff shouted up the stairs.

"Coming, Dad!" And about five minutes later Maggie came running down the stairs, freshly showered with a duffel bag in tow.

"That's a mighty big bag for one night. Are you planning on leaving me?"

Maggie smiled. "Never! But I did pack some of Mom's old photo albums, the ones with horses. I thought Katie would like to see them. She is going to show me photos of her dad and his horse. Did you know that Katie's dad died about two years ago?"

Jeff frowned. "No, I guess things have been hard on Katie and her mom as well. Maybe they can give me some advice."

Maggie hugged her dad. "You're doing just fine."

With that, Maggie ran out the door to the car.

"Mom! They're here!" yelled Katie. "Mom!"

"I hear you, Katie. Last time I checked, you knew how to open the door."

Katie threw the door open, and Maggie practically tumbled into the foyer.

"Come in, guys. Hi, Mr. Thompson, this is my mom, Olivia." Katie's mom was walking into the foyer, wiping her hands on a dish towel. Jeff stuck his hand out to her.

"Hello, Olivia. I'm Jeff. I am so pleased to meet you. Maggie and Katie have become fast friends."

Olivia shook Jeff's hand and said, "Come on in, Jeff. I've made a salad, and the pizza is on its way. We have plenty, and I would love for you to join us."

Jeff smiled and blushed. "I'd love to."

The girls exchanged looks and ran upstairs to Katie's room.

After dinner, they all got up and started clearing the table together. "Well, Olivia, that was the best pizza I've had in a long time. And the salad…the salad was fantastic."

Maggie rolled her eyes. "Dad!"

Katie and Olivia laughed, and Jeff reached out and gave Maggie a big hug.

"You have a great night, kiddo, and get some sleep. I'll pick you up from the barn after your lesson tomorrow."

"Okay, Dad, I love you." Maggie hugged her dad.

"I love you too, kiddo," Jeff said as he hugged her back. "Olivia, I had a wonderful time."

Olivia smiled back at him. "Me too, Jeff. Thanks for letting Maggie stay over."

With that, Jeff waved and walked through the night to his car.

The girls giggled as they made a nest on the floor. They dragged every comforter and pillow into a pile. Olivia had prepared hot cocoa with marshmallows, and they were snuggled in for a night of photo albums and pony talk.

ᑌᑌᑌ

"My dad's name was Tyler, and he had me on a pony as early as I can remember," said Katie. "He would tell me stories of magical ponies who could talk and fly. Only nobody could hear or see them fly unless they 'knew.' They only talked inside their owners' heads. Seem silly to you?" Katie looked at Maggie slyly out of the corner of her eye.

Maggie laughed a little uncomfortably. "Yeah. Silly." She was thinking of the times she swore she had heard Bella speaking in her head. She was also remembering the day Willow and Ms. Cavalieri had literally soared over that fallen tree. But she was sure that she hadn't seen wings.

"Okay, time for the pictures!" said Katie as she reached over Maggie to grab her photo album. "Yours first or mine?"

Maggie shrugged. "Doesn't matter; let's look at yours. I can't wait to see your dad and Dance."

So the girls squished together and opened the first album.

Pictures of a smiling boy beaming up at them, with Katie's big, brown eyes, made Maggie smile instantly. They reminded her of her new best friend. Even his pony looked like Lily. There were pictures of him grooming his pony, pictures of him showing, and pictures of him jumping Cross Country.

"Wow! What fun!" Maggie exclaimed. "Is this the same pony?" Maggie asked, pointing to a picture of what looked like the same pony, but obviously Tyler and the pony were older and bigger.

"Yes, all these pictures are of Dance." Maggie looked at her and then back at the album, flipping through the pages. As she flipped through, she noticed a picture of Katie's dad and someone else fencing. *Fencing.* That brought back a vague memory of something. The dark-haired boy he was fencing was taller than Tyler, and even in this grainy picture, she could tell that he wore a smirk on his face. *Why is fencing in a photo album of ponies?* As she closely studied the pictures, something else caught her eye: the girls sitting on the sidelines watching. She couldn't quite see their faces, but something, something looked very familiar. She turned the pages quickly.

"Wait!" She flipped forward, looking at photos of a teenage Tyler again. "Wait!" There he was, smiling right at her, each arm around a teenage girl. Both girls were laughing, eyes sparkling. "Katie! Katie!" Maggie could not believe her eyes—the girl on the left was a young, happy Ms. Cavalieri. The girl on the right that was smiling into the camera was Sarah, Maggie's mom!

"So you mean to tell me that my mom, your dad, and Ms. Cavalieri all knew each other?" said Maggie, still wide-eyed.

"Yes. And some of the other girls' parents, too," said Katie. "They practically grew up together."

Maggie was flipping through her mom's photo album now, amazed that it had all been in front of her the whole time. She turned to Katie. "How long have you known?"

"We all knew the day your dad brought you in for the first time," said Katie. "You complete our team."

"Why didn't you guys say anything?"

Katie smiled. "What were we going to say? We wanted you to join us because you liked us, not because your mom rode here."

Maggie was thoughtful. "Katie, tell me something, how is it that Bella is related to Chloe, and Lily is related to Dance…and we ended up with these ponies?"

Katie took a sip of her hot cocoa before answering. "Well, they are all related, and they always find their way to us. We are destined to be with our ponies. Couldn't you feel it? The pull? The feeling that Bella was yours?"

Maggie nodded, too stunned to say anything. How in the heck did she fall into this magical pony world? *Wow! This will certainly be an adventure to remember!*

CHAPTER SEVEN

The Storm

T he next day at the barn was a new experience for Maggie. She was looking at all the kids and ponies through different eyes. Bella seemed even happier than usual to see her. She was nickering and rubbing her head on Maggie so hard that it almost knocked her over.

"What's gotten into you, Bella?" Maggie asked while vigorously rubbing Bella just under her thick forelock.

"She knows," said Katie as she entered Lily's stall. "Lily told her."

Maggie frowned, still finding it hard to believe that she and her pony were going to form some sort of magical bond that would allow them to communicate. Bella snorted and shook her head in disbelief.

"Give me a break, Bella. Until last night I had no idea that you could actually understand my thoughts. I still don't know if I will ever be able to return the favor. Be patient with me, please." Maggie laughed as Bella shook her head again and started searching her pockets. "I know what that means." Maggie laughed again as she removed an apple from her pocket.

"Maggie, do you want to hack the ponies in the back field again today? We can practice jumping the little ditch out there. It will get us ready for Cross Country."

"Yes! Then we can take a little rest by the stream and have a snack. The grass looked like it's starting to turn really green down there, so I'm guessing the ponies would like a little snack as well." Both ponies snorted in response.

They quickly groomed and tacked the ponies and stuffed their jacket pockets with snacks that were appropriate for little girls as well as ponies. As they stepped up to the mounting block, Ms. Cavalieri walked over to them.

"Good morning, Maggie. I trust you had a good evening with Katie? Was it, uh, enlightening?" Ms. Cavalieri shot a glance at Katie.

"Katie showed me her photo albums. I didn't know that you knew my mom. That you were actually friends with her." Maggie looked searchingly into Ms. Cavalieri's eyes.

"Yes, Maggie. I grew up with Sarah. She was like a sister to me. One day we will have this conversation, but today go out and enjoy your pony." Ms. Cavalieri looked up at the sky and added, "Don't stay out too long—the sky isn't looking great today."

Maggie looked up at a clear, blue, sunny sky.

"And, Katie…no jumping ditches. Lily will tell me if you do." Lily snorted and shook her head at Ms. Cavalieri.

The girls exchanged guilty looks as they mounted their ponies and headed out toward the back field.

"Don't worry, Maggie, Lily can't really talk to anyone but me. But she does tend to have a guilty look when we've bent the rules a bit. Come on! Race you!" With that Katie and Lily sped off at a gallop. Maggie laughed and Bella raced after them.

∪◡∪

The girls were resting in the sun, leaning against their saddles, and eating the last of their granola bars. The ponies were grazing nearby, keeping an occasional watchful eye on their girls.

"I love that we can take their bridles and saddles off and let them relax," said Maggie. "That's yet another plus in having a magic pony." She giggled as she said it. *Magic pony. Will I ever get used to saying that?*

They had managed to "accidentally" jump over some logs and a ditch or two. Riding her pony was an entirely new experience knowing that Bella could read her mind. She could trust her to do what she wanted, and it made her a better rider. Not such a micromanager. Maggie didn't know where she came up with that word, but it had been in her head today for the first half of the ride. Finally she managed to sit and enjoy the ride, and the world went away. She was starting to think that Bella may have actually been calling her a micromanager. *Hmmm.* She'd have to think about that during lessons. She had mentioned it to Katie, who told her that—as long as her requests were clear—she wouldn't need to micromanage, and she could trust that her pony would do what she wanted. *Trust. That word has come up several times at the barn.*

"We better start heading home." Maggie must have been dozing because Katie's voice startled her a bit. "Look at the sky. I swear, Ms. Cavalieri is always right."

The ponies came trotting over to the girls and stood still while the girls started tacking them up. As they were tightening the girths, the wind started to really pick up. By the time they had the bridles on, the sky was almost completely dark, and the wind was whipping the trees around like they were small weeds.

"Get on! Let's go!" shouted Katie above the wind. "This can't be good!"

Bella was galloping before Maggie could even get her feet into the stirrups. *Hang on!* That was Bella; Maggie was sure that was Bella! She leaned forward and clung to her pony and sat as still as she could so that her pony could run as fast as needed.

It was raining now, pouring. *How could this storm come up so quickly? Without warning?* It was almost as if it was forced. It just didn't seem natural. It was raining so hard that Maggie could barely see Lily's rump in front of her. She squinted and leaned closer to Bella's neck.

All of a sudden, something swooped out of the sky in front of Bella! *Was that a bird? It was huge!* Bella kept running, but within a few strides, it swept by again. The second time, Bella had to pull up a bit to keep from hitting it.

Katie looked over her shoulder and yelled, "Don't stop! Keep running!"

Bella started running again, but the giant bird came at them a third time! This time, as Bella pulled up, she stumbled. Maggie grabbed at Bella's neck for support but saw the ground coming up fast instead. She hit the ground hard, and right before everything went black, she heard her pony screaming.

"Maggie! Maggie! Get up! I need you to get up, Maggie!" Maggie could hear Ms. Cavalieri but couldn't make her eyes respond. "Maggie, open your eyes and get up right now. I need you to help me."

Maggie opened her eyes slowly. It felt as if she had been laying there forever, but unfortunately it was still storming around her. She sat up quickly, suddenly remembering everything. "Bella! Where's Bella?"

"Can you get up?" Ms. Cavalieri looked concerned, and Maggie could see Lily dancing around behind her with Katie looking around anxiously.

"Yes. I'm fine. Where's Bella?" Maggie was starting to feel sick now.

"Come on, let me help you onto Willow. We have to get out of this storm. Now." Ms. Cavalieri practically hoisted her up on her own and threw her onto Willow's back. Willow was snorting nervously but stood perfectly still while

Ms. Cavalieri got on behind Maggie. "Let's go!" With that command, both horses whirled and galloped, top speed, back toward the farm.

"I know, Willow, they have what they want right now, so they are not following us. But we need to get back all the same. We are not prepared for a fight yet." Ms. Cavalieri was having her own personal conversation with her horse while they were galloping through a storm. *But where is my pony?*

By the time they reached the barn, many of the girls were out front, opening the barn doors and reaching for Maggie. They all seemed calm, but their eyes told another story. Nobody asked about Bella. As they pulled Maggie off Willow, Maggie burst into tears. "Where is Bella?! Why won't anyone talk to me? Katie? Katie, are you okay?"

Katie wrapped her arms around Maggie. "Maggie, I was so scared that you were hurt. Thank goodness you're okay. Don't worry, we will find Bella." She looked questioningly at Ms. Cavalieri.

"Maggie, Sam and Lyndsey will take care of the horses. Come with me. I think I have some hot cocoa in my office, and I certainly have some explaining to do." Sam and Lyndsey rushed forward, taking Lily and Willow and walking them to the wash rack, talking in quiet, soothing voices.

The other girls parted as they walked down the barn aisle to Ms. Cavalieri's office. Katie grabbed Bella's and Lily's blankets off of their stalls as they walked by and draped one over Maggie's shoulders. Maggie could smell the warm, dusty smell that belonged to Bella, and she felt the tears rising and that familiar lump in her throat. *It isn't fair. It just isn't fair.* Hadn't Maggie lost enough? This was the one thing, the one thing that made Maggie feel close to her mother. When she rode, she knew that her mother had done the exact same things on a pony that was as much like Bella as possible. She couldn't face losing Bella now.

As they walked into the warm, dimly lit office, Ms. Cavalieri looked over at Maggie and said, "Don't worry, Maggie, I will do everything possible to get Bella back." She moved over to the little kitchen and pulled out some cocoa after she had lit the stove to boil some water. "Maggie, you remind me so much of Sarah. Sometimes it hurts me to look at you. Sometimes it brings me back to childhood, and I almost don't want to come back. Your mom was very funny, Maggie. She always laughed and made everyone around her laugh. She had an exceptional connection with the animals." Ms. Cavalieri smiled as she said this. She turned and poured them each a cup of hot cocoa. "We all have a unique connection with our own ponies, but your mom's was extra special. Sometimes I worried that she could communicate with all of our ponies and that she could talk them into playing funny tricks on us. She promised that was not the case, so I'm sure it wasn't. Above all, your mom was honest to a fault. She was adored by us all." Ms. Cavalieri sat down across from both girls. "What I am about to tell you is something that Katie and the other girls already know; it's the reason it was so important for you to find us and the reason it was so important for you and Bella to find each other. Maggie, we are and have been in a battle, a battle that we have to win. It has gone on for years, and it will go on forever, but we need you to help us continue this fight."

Maggie sat there, cup half-raised to her lips. As she looked around the office, she saw things she had never paid attention to before. On the wall hung a helmet, unlike one she had ever seen before. Why had she never noticed that it appeared to be made of some sort of metal rather than the usual velvet-looking helmet? Also, there was a foil hanging parallel to the floor in a silver rack. There was a silver rack below it that held no foil. There was a vest, a

Cross Country vest that was made out of the same funny metal as the helmet. *What is this place? Speechless. Warriors? This is just too much. I'm so tired. Tired of feeling sad. Tired of losing. Too much.*

"Maggie, are you okay?" Katie reached over and wrapped her arms around Maggie. "Please don't be scared. We are all in this together. We need each other."

"So you need me?" Maggie's voice was shaky. "You didn't *want* me. You didn't really *want* to be my best friend, but you *needed* me." Maggie shook Katie's arm off. "All of this," she threw her arms out, "all of this is crazy! What about my PONY?! Where is my PONY?!"

Ms. Cavalieri rose from her seat. "Maggie, of course we care for you. You are a part of us. You have been a part of us for centuries. We are bound together by something deeper than mere friendship. We are bound by trust. Absolute trust. We are able to defend this great magic because of this trust."

"Trust?" Maggie nearly shouted at Ms. Cavalieri. "How can I trust all of you if you keep hiding these crazy secrets from me? I need to know. I need to know everything. And we have to find Bella."

"Ms. Cavalieri," Katie spoke up, "they took Bella. But they didn't hurt her. I think they wanted us to know that she is unharmed. So that we will come and rescue her." Katie looked shaken up. "They know that we are complete now."

"Yes, they know we are complete, and they know that the best chance they have of defeating us is now. While we are young and inexperienced. We have to go now! Get Sam, Lyndsey, and Reece. Tell them to saddle up. It's time."

"What about me and Lily?" Katie looked nervous but not at all scared.

"Katie, don't you think that your pony has been through enough today? She has just seen her stall mate picked up and carried away by dragons. You need to go to her and comfort her. Maggie, it would be a good idea for you to be there too so that Lily knows you are not angry or disappointed in her." Ms. Cavalieri reached for her phone, obviously dismissing them.

"Wait? *Dragons?* You just can't send me out without explaining this. I am coming too, right?" Maggie was starting to feel frantic now.

"Maggie, I promise I will explain everything, but we have to act now if we are going to get your pony back alive. This is very important." Ms. Cavalieri took a deep breath. "I need your help though. I need you to focus on Bella. I need you to try to reach out to her mind and give her hope. You can do it. You need to reach out to her and calm her and let her know that we are coming for her and that we will save her. When you do this—Maggie, listen to me closely—when you do this, you will be transported to her. Not physically, but mentally. You will see her, and she will be able to see you, but you will not be seen by anyone else. You will not be in your physical body, so you will not be able to touch or move anything, but you can use your mind and your hope to make this rescue successful. Now go. Go to Bella and comfort her. I will let you know before we leave."

With this, Ms. Cavalieri turned her back to them and made a phone call. "Darren. Darren, we need you." They heard her say as they left the office.

CHAPTER EIGHT

Dragons

K atie slid the stall door open, and Lily immediately came to her and buried her head in Katie's chest. Katie wrapped her arms around her pony's head, and they stood there together silently. Maggie turned her back on her two new friends. She was sad for them, but she was also hurting for herself.

As she turned away, she realized that she was facing Bella's stall. At first all she wanted to do was run away from the emptiness, but something pulled her to it instead. She opened the door and looked around. The water buckets were clean and full, and there was a pile of hay in the corner. Everything was in order. Only, no pony. Maggie slid to the floor in the pile of hay, Bella's blanket still wrapped around her.

She closed her eyes and breathed in the smell of the hay and shavings. The very special smell of her pony. As she inhaled, she imagined that she could see Bella. She saw her standing there in that muddy paddock, waiting to be found. Waiting to be found by Maggie. Bella had known from the moment that she set eyes on Maggie that she was her human. Why hadn't Maggie seen it? Why did it take Maggie so long to realize that Bella was special? She remembered standing in this very stall, arms wrapped around her pony, feeling so warm and loved. Feeling what she knew her mother must have felt at her age with her arms wrapped around a very similar pony. As she sat there in the hay, in the too-quiet barn, she drifted off.

It was dark—dark and hot. She felt scared. As she looked around, she realized that she was no longer in the barn, but in some sort of a cave? Or something underground. There was very little light, but as she looked around, she realized that she was sitting in a pile of hay, leaning up against a rock wall. Just a few feet away from her was Bella! Bella! She wanted to scream. But something told her not to alarm the pony. Bella stood there tied to a metal ring in the ground, huge rusted chain around her neck.

Above them on a rock ledge sat a large bird. Bird? Upon looking closer, Maggie changed her mind. She wasn't quite sure what she was looking at anymore. It was something that was kind of in between a hawk and a small dragon. Its sharp eyes scanned over where she was sitting and rested on her for what seemed an eternity, but eventually the hawk thing looked away. Ms. Cavalieri had said that nobody would be able to see her; she hoped that meant this crazy creature couldn't see her either.

She sat there and focused on the trembling white pony. *Bella,* she whispered in her mind, *Bella, I'm here. I'm here.*

Bella's head jerked up as if Maggie had yelled at her, and hawk's head snapped around and looked sharply at Bella. Slowly it stretched its wings and flew off toward a dark tunnel.

Shhh. Don't make any sudden movements. Bella's nostrils flared, and her eyes got really big, but she did as she was told. *Can you see me?* Maggie asked.

Bella snorted and shook her head. Maggie stood and slowly moved toward Bella. She wrapped her arms around her pony's neck, and although she couldn't really feel her, she felt the warmth and was sure Bella felt it too.

"I'm going to get you out of here," Maggie whispered. "I don't know how, but Ms. Cavalieri has a plan. She says that they don't want to hurt you. Have they hurt you yet?" Bella shook her head again.

I'm scared. Maggie heard this as clearly as if someone had said it out loud to her, even though it was just Bella in her head. She smiled through her fear.

"I know you are, Bella. I'm scared too. But everything will be okay. Ms. Cavalieri says that you were carried away by dragons! Did they injure you? Did they want to hurt you? Where are they?" Bella turned her head toward the dark tunnel that was about eight feet away from them.

Maggie, they're not what you are thinking. They are like us—they are smart, and they have riders who can speak with them too. That was the most Maggie had ever heard from her pony. Their bond must be getting stronger. *They want a battle. They want us all to become like them.*

Maggie was confused. *Like them? Ponies and dragons are very different creatures.* Maggie didn't think that the dragons wanted the ponies to become like them but rather wanted to eat them. *That's what dragons do right? Eat things? Burn things? Destroy things?*

"Bella, how can they get in to rescue you? Where is the entrance?" Maggie was frantically looking around, but Bella simply looked up. As Maggie followed Bella's gaze, she realized the little bit of light was coming from high above. She could see a little opening in the cave. Did that make it a mountain? *Could Bella be inside a mountain cave? Well, that would be a good place for dragons.*

Just then, Bella's head jerked up! *Maggie, they're coming.*

"But they can't see or hear me, right?" whispered Maggie.

No, but they can feel you through me. Please back away. Try to go back to the others now and let them know I'm okay. Tell them that I'm in the last cave of the mountain range.

"I'm not leaving!" cried Maggie. "They know where you are, and they will come and get you! I'll stay here with you and do what I can to help!"

She heard footsteps, and she squinted hard into the dark tunnel. She saw a tall figure walk into the little bit of light provided by the opening in the top of the cave. A man, a man dressed in sparkling armor with the hawk sitting on his shoulder. Like something from Camelot, he looked brave and handsome, but familiar. Wait! It was the man from the horse sale. The tall, dark-haired man who tried to get her to buy the bay pony instead of Bella. *Mr. Stephen!* She heard footsteps behind him and tried to blend deeper into the shadows, even though she knew that he couldn't see her. *Those weren't footsteps! Those were hoof steps!* Following Stephen was a giant horse! This was no ordinary horse; this was a massive horse that appeared to have been covered in some sort of armor that resembled Stephen's armor. The armor shimmered in the darkness and looked almost alive. Wait! That wasn't armor at all; it was some sort of scales! Dragons! These weren't the dragons of the stories and tales Maggie had heard! These were horses!

At that very moment, the "dragon" snorted, and smoke blew out of his nostrils. He shook his giant head, and his eyes glimmered yellow!

She could see Bella dancing and pulling on the rusted chain, and she could see the fear in her eyes. She leapt for her pony and landed face-first in a pile of shavings. She was back at Blackwatch Stables. In Bella's stall.

Without thinking, she jumped up and ran toward the office. "Ms. Cavalieri!" The ponies all jerked their heads up as she ran by their stalls. "Ms. Cavalieri! I know where she is; I've seen Bella!"

Ms. Cavalieri was in the doorway of her office. "We think we know where she is as well.

The dragons live inside a mountain range. We know this. We know where it is too. The problem is how to get Bella when they are expecting us. They want a fight, and I am just not sure that our young warriors are ready. I am waiting for Mr. McMillan to show up. He is the head instructor and owner of McMillan Stables. It's a place much like ours. Together we can be better prepared to rescue Bella."

Maggie stood there in awe. "You mean that there are more stables like this?"

"Yes, Maggie. You didn't think that we were the only stable in the whole world with magical horses and ponies, did you?" Ms. Cavalieri marched back into her office and sat down at her desk.

Uh, yes, Maggie thought as she looked at Ms. Cavalieri as if she were nuts.

"Well, Darren—Mr. McMillan to you—will be here soon, and then we can put our plan together. Maggie, not a word to your father. He doesn't need to know all of this. I doubt that Sarah ever told him the truth, and I think this would send him over the edge. I am not trying to teach you to lie to your father, but let's simply protect him from the truth for a while. If he ever asks you if your pony is magical, please feel free to tell him the truth."

Huh, like that would happen, thought Maggie.

"Ms. Cavalieri," Maggie said cautiously, "I think I saw a dragon. It looked just like a horse."

"Yes, Maggie. A dragon is not like we imagine. It's not the mythical flying, fire-breathing lizard as we have been led to believe; it is a horse," said Ms. Cavalieri sadly.

"But how in the world can a horse be bad? What can lead a horse into a life of being evil?" asked Maggie. She was thinking of Bella and all the ponies she had come to know in the recent months and simply couldn't imagine one that was evil.

"Maggie, the ponies and horses are bonded to their owners forever. They are an extension, a part of their owners. When an owner is good, the pony is good. But if something turns the owner the wrong way...well, the pony becomes a part of that as well. They are loyal. Through good and bad. These ponies will always, always reflect who we are. If our hearts harden, our horses' hearts do also. But they harden physically as well. It helps them serve us better."

CHAPTER NINE

Breaking the Rules

Sam came bursting into the office. "Ms. Cavalieri, we are all tacked up and ready to go."

She was definitely not wearing the "usual" riding attire. She was wearing black breeches and a black shirt, but she was also wearing a vest like the one in Ms. Cavalieri's office, which looked almost like metal and was similar to the armor worn by the man in the mountain's cave.

It looked as if she was wearing chaps made of the same shiny metal material that covered her from her waist down her thighs and down the front and side of her calves. Lyndsey and Reece were behind her and dressed the exact same way, metal helmets tucked under their arms.

"Thank you, Sam," said Ms. Cavalieri. "Make sure that Jazz, Shooter, and Athena are tacked up and armored as well, and please get Willow prepared for me."

"Yes, ma'am," the girls said in unison. None of them looked nervous or scared but simply ready and serious.

"Wait, girls." She opened a large closet that held several of the slim swords. She threw one to Sam, one to Reece, and one to Lyndsey, who caught them as if she was tossing them a Frisbee. The girls rushed out of the room. Ms. Cavalieri slowly walked to the foil hanging on the wall and took it for herself. She paused for just a moment before the empty rack. "Go help the others," Ms. Cavalieri said without turning to them.

Maggie blindly followed the other girls through the barn, wondering what they were going to ask her to do. *Will they give me the opportunity to save my own chosen pony?*

The barn doors burst open! Maggie jumped, and the other girls turned in surprise. Standing in the middle of the aisle was a tall man dressed in armor that was much like what Sam and the other girls wore with the longest-legged horse she had ever seen by his side.

"Ladies," the man said with one eyebrow cocked, "I assume Erin is here somewhere?"

As he walked closer to them, Maggie could see that while the man was quite handsome, he had a snooty look on his face that made Maggie dislike him a bit. In fact, as her eyes moved over to his tall, long-legged steed, she noticed that the dark bay was exactly like his owner. His small, chiseled face was covered by a thick forelock that stuck out of the armored browband. His large nostrils were flared, but somehow it looked as if they were flared in the same manner that his owner had cocked his eyebrow...almost in distaste. Like they were too good for Blackwatch Stables.

"Coal, wait here while I find Erin. Hopefully these young ladies can find you a clean bucket of water." The horse snorted and stomped his hoof impatiently. "I'll be right back."

With that, the stranger walked straight toward Ms. Cavalieri's office and walked right in the door.

"That was Darren. Or Mr. McMillan," said Sam with a combination of awe and distaste. Reece sighed and Lyndsey snorted, sounding much like the horse Coal did earlier. "And obviously Erin is Ms. Cavalieri. She hates it when he just walks into her office without knocking."

"I don't know why he thinks he is so much better than us. Last year at the games we kicked his students' butts!" Lyndsey threw a dirty look toward the office. "Let's get this nag some water." Coal reached over and bit Lyndsey right on the arm. Maggie heard the loud *thunk* of Shooter kicking the stall in protest. "Easy, Shooter," Lyndsey called over her shoulder. "You'll get your chance." The pony gave a short neigh in return.

Sam ran off to finish getting Willow ready, and Maggie walked back to Bella's stall. Katie was still there with Lily.

"Maggie, it's going to be fine. I wish that Lily and I could go with the rest of them. We are ready!" Katie sounded desperate. "After all, it's my fault that Bella was taken in the first place. If I hadn't insisted that we go to the back field…if I hadn't stayed out there so long, knowing that Ms. Cavalieri warned me…" Lily shoved her head into Katie's chest as if she needed some comfort of her own. "No, Lily, you couldn't have gone after her, they would have taken us all then."

"Katie, don't be silly. This is absolutely not your fault," Maggie said and then looked thoughtfully at Katie. "Katie, do you and Lily really think that you are ready for battle?"

Katie looked at Maggie slyly. "Are you thinking what I'm thinking?"

"I think so," said Maggie, "but I don't even know where the mountain is, and even if I did, I am not sure how to get into it."

Lily snorted and looked right at Katie. "Lily knows," Katie said softly. "Lily knows how to get there."

Maggie felt a jump in her stomach. "Let's get ready!"

Together, the girls ran to the tack room.

"Maggie, Katie, where are you going?" Ms. Cavalieri snapped at them.

"We were going to see if we could help the girls prepare," said Katie with a perfectly straight face. Maggie took care not to look right at Ms. Cavalieri.

"No need. We are all ready to go. We should be back in a few hours. In the meantime, try to comfort Lily. I know that she is quite upset. Keep the barn doors closed and don't try anything sneaky!" Ms. Cavalieri stared down at them and Maggie shifted uneasily.

With that, she turned on her heel and left them standing there with their guilty consciences.

Sam, Lyndsey, and Reece walked through the barn, leading their ponies, serious looks on their faces. They led their ponies right out into the courtyard where Ms. Cavalieri and Mr. McMillan waited with Willow and Coal. Willow seemed to be intent on ignoring the tall bay while he pranced in one place, looking very impressive and very stuck-up.

"Mount up, ladies," said Mr. McMillan. "Let's go rescue a pony."

They all mounted up, looking very formidable in their armor. They no longer looked like girls and ponies but rather war horses of some sort. All the ponies were now prancing and pawing the ground. They were ready, and they knew their job.

Before Maggie knew what was going on, they all spun in unison and galloped off toward the back field. No one stopped to open a gate; instead, each one soared over the fence. To Maggie's great surprise, none of them ever touched the ground again! She turned in amazement to Katie, who was watching them intently.

"What?!" That was all that escaped Maggie's lips.

"Come on, Maggie, you knew they could fly, now you've seen it. Let's go!"

They raced into the barn. "Maggie, grab Lily, and I'll get the tack," Katie yelled over her shoulder as she ran past Lily's stall and to the tack room.

Maggie opened Lily's stall, and Lily was right in her way, ready to go. "Okay, Lily, let me get your halter on…"

"Don't bother," said Katie, who was now standing right behind Maggie, "she knows what's going on. She won't go anywhere." Katie handed Maggie a small armored bridle, and she looked at the saddle briefly and put it on the saddle rack. "I'm not even going to bother with the saddle since we will be riding double. It will be easier if we are bareback. Here, Maggie, put both of these chest plates on Lily so that we will have an extra for Bella. What's wrong with you? Move!"

Maggie was just standing there with her mouth open. *This is going to be super dangerous.* Maggie wasn't sure if she was really ready to put her best friend and Lily in such danger.

Katie looked at her as if she was reading her mind. "Pull it together, Maggie. This is what we were born to do. We will be fine. Lily understands the danger, and she wouldn't want it any other way."

Katie raced to Ms. Cavalieri's office; Maggie followed close behind. She ripped open the closet, tossing Maggie a helmet and vest before grabbing one of her own. She paused, looking at the foils.

"Katie, do you even know how to use one of those? You could cut your own hand off." Maggie was looking anxiously at Katie.

"Well, we need some sort of weapon, and I have had a few lessons. Do you want one?" Katie pulled one from a rack.

Maggie shook her head, too stunned to answer. She didn't have any idea how to even hold one. Did she? Looking at the foil up close, it felt familiar somehow. "No, I don't want one," said Maggie decisively, and they raced out of the office together.

Maggie pulled on the armored vest and helmet.

"Make sure your hair is tucked in well." Katie smirked. "Ms. Cavalieri would be so disappointed if we didn't look good while breaking all the rules."

Maggie gave a little nervous giggle and buckled her chin strap. "Okay. I'm ready!"

Katie led Lily out of the barn and over to the mounting block. She hopped on first and motioned for Maggie to get on behind.

"Won't we be too heavy for her?" Maggie asked.

Lily snorted and gave her a dirty look. "Guess not."

Maggie stepped up on the mounting block and swung her leg over the pony. She settled in right up close to Katie and put her arms around Katie's waist.

"Hang on, Maggie!" Katie said over her shoulder. "We are in for one of the greatest adventures of our lives...so far."

Lily spun on her haunches and galloped top speed toward the fence. Maggie felt Lily gather herself underneath them, and she squeezed her eyes shut tight. She heard Katie giggling and opened her eyes to see the ground falling away below them.

CHAPTER TEN

Dragon Mountain

T he ground sped by at an unreal pace. Maggie buried her face in Katie's back and held on tight. After about an hour, she felt Lily slow down a bit.

"What's wrong?" Maggie yelled in Katie's ear. "Is she getting tired?"

"No," Katie shouted back, "we are almost there! Get ready to buckle up for a landing!"

She hugged Katie even tighter and wondered if Katie was even aware of the danger that lay ahead. She pictured her Bella chained up in that cave, and it gave her courage. She had to rescue her pony! They had to find a way to bring Bella home safely.

She felt Lily getting slower and slower and watched the ground get closer. Sure enough, they were approaching a mountain range.

They landed just at the bottom of the mountain, and Maggie slid to the ground, legs shaking.

"Now what?" Maggie asked. She had not even thought this far. *Where are the others? Are they inside fighting that evil man and his dragon horse? What if they are injured? Or worse? What if they failed? We have to get in there to help! I just have to get to Bella!*

"Okay, so let's think this out," said Katie, interrupting Maggie's panicked thoughts. "The first thing that we have to do is get inside the mountain cave without anyone seeing us." Lily snorted, and the girls looked at her. "Lily says she knows a way in, but it will be a tight fit. She says it's a small tunnel that only ponies can fit through. Not horses."

"Well, that's good to know because that dragon thing was huge!" remembered Maggie. "Certainly couldn't fit through a pony-sized tunnel."

Lily shook her head and snorted again.

"Oh, well, one problem. We don't exactly know how close this tunnel will take us to Bella. Or even where exactly it goes," said Katie after looking intently at her pony.

"Well, we'll just have to see. Are you sure that you two don't want to stay outside and keep watch?" Maggie was worried about her friends.

"Are you kidding me? You just want to have all the fun." Katie winked and turned to Lily. "Show us the way."

The pony turned and started picking her way through the rocky terrain. They walked up and down the ridges of the mountain, following the black pony tail until Lily stopped. Katie rushed to the front, and sure enough, there was a small cave in front of them. They wouldn't have even noticed it if Lily hadn't led them there. Katie and Maggie started clearing rocks away from the entrance, and as they did, they saw that it would be big enough for them to fit through with Lily.

"Lily, seriously, you should stay here and be our get-away pony," said Maggie. "They are far more likely to notice us if we have a pony following us through the caves."

Lily snorted and looked at Katie, obviously unhappy with what Maggie said.

Katie patted Lily on the neck. "You know, Lily, she has a point. You are not known for being quiet. And we may need you to be ready to go when we get out with Bella." Lily put her sweet, dark face into Katie's chest, and Katie's dark braids swung forward toward the pony. Katie quietly removed the extra breastplate from Lily and strapped it to her own back like a backpack. "Nothing will happen to me. Besides, they would want you more than they want me. Please trust me and stay out here." Lily snorted and stood still with her head hanging as the girls started their trek toward the center of the mountain. She gave a quiet whinny, and Katie turned and waved at her.

Maggie felt as if she had been walking in a crouched position forever. In reality, they had probably only been in the tunnel for about twenty minutes.

"Katie, do you see light yet?" Maggie tried to see around Katie.

"Nothing; it's so dark." Katie was starting to sound discouraged too.

At that very moment, Katie tumbled to the ground and disappeared.

"Katie!" Maggie whispered as loud as she dared. "Katie, are you okay?"

As she said that, she tumbled forward and down and landed right smack on top of Katie.

"I was fine until you landed on me," grunted Katie.

"Sorry. Where are we now?" Maggie looked around as she got to her feet and held out a hand for Katie.

"I don't know; I was kind of hoping you would know," Katie said, eyes bright with excitement. "This is crazy!"

Maggie saw that they were in a small room that was lit with torches that were stuck into the stone walls. They blinked their eyes, trying to adjust to the dim light.

"Do you hear that?" asked Maggie. "I hear breathing, I think." She whirled around, trying to take everything in and worried that there was someone else in the cave with them.

"*Shh.* Yes, I hear it," whispered Katie. "Look! Across the room!"

Maggie stared for a moment, seeing nothing. Then the shadows began to take shape. Ponies! Ponies huddled together in the dark in the far corner of the room. There were probably five or six of them.

The girls walked slowly side by side toward the ponies. They just stood there, heads up and ears pricked, watching the girls approach.

Maggie reached in her pocket and drew out a treat. The pony in the front slowly walked toward her. As the white pony approached, Maggie took in the small herd. They were rugged. They looked older, and she realized that they were a bit larger than a pony. They were actually horses. The white horse closest to her slowly reached out and took the treat.

"Easy," Maggie said. "What are all of you doing here?" The white horse snorted quietly and shook her head. "How long have you been here?"

The horse blinked at her, and at that moment, Maggie thought she heard, "Years, child. Years."

Maggie stroked the horse on her face, and as she did so, something made her lift the thick forelock. She noticed that there was something familiar about that face; she stared hard, trying to make out the marking. As she stared, her finger automatically traced the marking on the mare's face. It was shaped like a…

Katie grabbed Maggie's arm. "We have to find Bella! Come on!" With this, the white horse jerked her head up and looked right at Maggie.

Go! Go get Bella; we'll be okay.

Maggie looked at Katie. "Did you hear that?"

"What?" asked Katie.

"The horse spoke to me," said Maggie.

"That's impossible," Katie said. Maggie looked at Katie like she was crazy. "Well, you know what I mean. It's impossible for you to hear her unless this were your horse, and we know that Bella is yours."

The white horse pushed Maggie, hard.

"Come on, Maggie, I think she's telling us to go," said Katie.

"Yes, but where? Where do we go now?" asked Maggie, looking into the white horse's eyes. "Do you know?"

The horse walked toward the darkest part of the cave. The other horses started shifting uncomfortably, as if they were afraid of that part of the cave. As Maggie and Katie neared that end, they noticed that the tunnel continued. But it was closed off by large branches that were placed into the walls of the cave, creating a fence to block the tunnel. The girls climbed through the fence and looked back at the small herd of horses.

"We will come back for you!" Maggie whispered. "I promise!" With that, the girls slipped back into darkness, once again following a stone tunnel that would lead them to the next step of their adventure.

This tunnel was much taller, so they could move faster than they did through the first one. They slowed a bit as they approached what looked to be another cave at the end of the passageway. They stood in the shadows of the tunnel, looking around the cave. They gasped in amazement!

"Have you ever seen or imagined anything like this?" asked Katie, looking around with her mouth open.

"Oh my. No way!" Maggie stared in amazement. They were standing in a giant cave that was lit by beautiful torchlight. It appeared that the middle was almost like a courtyard, and surrounding it were magnificent stalls. They were giant stalls; Maggie could only assume that this is where the giant horses lived. The stalls gleamed a dull bronze. All of the stalls were empty, thank goodness.

"Holy cow! Look at the size of those stalls!" Katie gasped wide-eyed, looking at Maggie. "Imagine the size of the horses!"

"Dragons," said Maggie, "imagine the size of the dragons. And where are they?"

"I don't know, but I'm glad they're not here!" said Katie.

"Yes. But where?" said Maggie, looking around. "We need to be extra careful! These guys are huge, and it looks like there are quite a few of them!"

Katie placed her finger over her lips and then pointed up. Nesting above them on top of the stalls were three of the hawks. They appeared to be in a trance, as if they were looking through the stone walls at something Maggie and Katie couldn't see.

"Well, Maggie, there are three ways out, not including the way we came. Which way should we go?" Katie was starting to look worried now, one eye on the dragon-hawks and one eye on the tunnels.

"Give me a moment." Maggie closed her eyes and thought about Bella. She tuned out Katie's nervous breathing and the magical stable around her. She thought of the special pony smell that belonged to Bella.

"This way!" Maggie jogged off toward the tunnel on the far left. "Come on!"

Katie shrugged and followed.

Behind them, unnoticed, the hawks left their perches and flew swiftly down another tunnel.

CHAPTER ELEVEN

The Battle

As they quickly made their way through the tunnel, they heard noises coming from a distance. They stopped, frozen in place.

"Do you think that's coming from the direction we are going?" whispered Katie.

Maggie shrugged. "I don't know. I sure hope not. It sounds like…" Maggie cocked her head to the side, listening closely.

Katie did the same. A split second later, they both looked at each other, eyes wide!

"A battle!" they said in unison.

"They are fighting each other! Our stable and this crazy dragon stable! We must go help!" cried Maggie.

"Wait!" said Katie, for once being the voice of reason. "They are great riders. We can't just go barging in there. We could be a major distraction, and someone on our side could get hurt!"

Maggie nodded, and they continued quickly and silently through the tunnel. As the sound of clashing swords and scraping hooves got louder, they slowed down. They crept quietly ahead until they reached the end of the tunnel. It opened up into a gigantic arena, probably three times bigger than the arena at Blackwatch Stables. As their vision adjusted to the light of the torches, they couldn't believe their eyes! There in front of them was not only the dark-haired man, Stephen, on his giant dragon, but there were three more of those dragons.

"Katie!" whispered a frantic Maggie, "how in the world are our girls going to get out of this in one piece?"

Katie shook her head, mouth open wide. "I have no idea. We have to help!" As she said that, a shiny, silver-colored dragon was sent flying across the cave by Sam and Jazz. Jazz looked like she was on fire, her chestnut coat glowing in the dull light. Something in her expression caught Maggie's attention. Jazz's eyes and expression matched that of the silver dragon—she looked positively deadly. Sam was in two-point, foil raised and ready to defend her horse. The silver horse and his rider did not go after Sam and Jazz but rather stood by the wall, sides heaving, trying to catch their breath.

Katie grabbed Maggie's arm in alarm. "Look!" Maggie looked up in time to see a dark dragon charging right at Lyndsey and Shooter. The dragon rammed into Shooter, who screamed in anger and pain as he stumbled to the ground. Lyndsey was knocked off, and Katie and Maggie sprinted across the cave to her. They reached her just as the dragon turned, pawing with eyes glowing. Maggie reached Lyndsey first and grabbed her hand, pulling her up just as the dragon made another charge for them. As they stood there, transfixed by the strong creature that was charging at them, Lyndsey lifted her foil and pushed the younger girls behind her. Maggie closed her eyes as the pounding of the hooves echoed in her ears. She heard the crashing of two bodies meeting, and as she opened her eyes, she saw Shooter throwing his body against the dark dragon with all his might. The dragon stood his ground for just a moment but then tumbled to the floor. His rider rolled away and didn't get up. The dragon leapt to his feet and stood over his rider and never made another move toward any of the Blackwatch riders.

"Go!" yelled Lyndsey. "Get out of here! Shooter, get them out of here!" The bay pony turned and galloped toward Maggie and Katie, who naturally ran away from the charging pony. He slid to a stop in front of them, tossing his head and pushing them toward one of the opposite tunnels. Shooter—normally the sweetest pony in the barn—was totally no-nonsense at the moment, and he wasn't going to take "no" for an answer. Over his shoulder they could see Reece and Athena doing what looked like a dance as they maneuvered away from the silver dragon. Reece was tall and elegant on her very large pony. Foil flickering in the candlelight, she looked as if she were modeling some new-age metal clothing instead of fighting a small army of dragons.

Mr. McMillan and Coal were actually in the air in a fierce battle with the dark-haired man and his massive dragon. The four of them seemed to be having the time of their lives. Both men had large, heavy swords, and their steeds were twisting and turning to avoid flying swords and hooves. Horse and dragon—with mouths wide open and hooves striking—were locked in combat.

Ms. Cavalieri spun Willow in a circle and spotted the two girls who were trapped on one side of the cave by the angry Shooter.

"Maggie! Katie! What the heck? Your pony! Go find her!" Ms. Cavalieri yelled while keeping a watchful eye on the fight. "Shooter, take care of them! I'll get Lyndsey!"

The bay pony spun and herded the girls into the tunnel. As they ran from the angry pony, they heard the sounds of armor clashing.

CHAPTER TWELVE

Rescued

As they reached the end, Maggie immediately recognized it as the tunnel in Bella's cave that Maggie had seen the dragon walk through. She knew that Bella was probably just steps away!

They walked into the cave, eyes adjusting to the little bit of light that was provided by the opening above. They didn't hear anything. Was Bella still even there? Maggie was searching the cave but couldn't see well enough to locate Bella.

"Bella?" whispered Maggie, holding tightly to Katie's hand. "Bella, we've come for you." They heard the scraping sound of metal on stone. "Bella?"

Then as they moved closer to the sound, they saw her. Bella. Her head was hanging, and her eyes were glazed over. She didn't even seem to hear them approaching. Shooter stopped and stood still as if guarding the tunnel.

Maggie's heart stuck in her throat as she started to run toward her pony. Katie grabbed her. "Wait," Katie whispered, "let's make sure this is not a trap. Make sure that we are alone."

They scanned the cave and didn't see or hear anything. Maggie and Katie moved slowly toward Bella. Suddenly Bella's head jerked up!

Maggie! The single word rang in Maggie's head. *You're really here?*

Maggie threw her arms around her pony's neck, breathing in the sweet pony smells and holding onto the warmth. "Bella, I'm here. I told you that we would come for you. Now we just have to figure out how to sneak you out of here. I don't think that you are strong enough to fly us both out through the top." Bella snorted in agreement.

"Do you think we can sneak her out through the tunnels? The way we came in?" asked Katie, looking nervously around her.

"I think that's our only choice." Maggie looked at Katie and took a deep breath. "Bella, we have to be super quiet."

"Don't forget this." Katie swung the armored breastplate from her back and fastened it to Bella.

Bella snorted and looked at Maggie. *My chain,* Maggie heard in her head.

"Oh, I forgot about that. How are we going to get that chain off of her?" Maggie looked to Katie for any ideas.

Shooter snorted and reared, suddenly at attention as he backed toward the girls and the pony.

"You won't have to worry about that, ladies." Both girls jumped at the sound of the man's voice. Standing in the mouth of the tunnel was Stephen and his tremendous dragon. "I knew you wouldn't be able to stay away, I just didn't think you would come so soon. I actually thought that you would be a little scared, like Sarah." He laughed, and as he did, a hawk landed on his shoulder.

"My mother wasn't scared of you! And I'm not scared of you either!" shouted Maggie, stepping in front of both Bella and Katie. "Wait, how do you know my mother?"

"Oh, Maggie, my dear, that is another story for another day. Don't worry, we will have plenty of time for stories. I even have a few stories for you, Katie. Tyler was a great rival. I will enjoy adding you and your ponies to my collection." As he walked closer to them,

Maggie, Katie, and Bella backed up, looking around for a miracle, for a way to escape.

"Don't worry, ladies, my warriors are finishing off your friends; you won't have to worry about them for long." As he moved closer to them, he reached to his side and pulled out a long silver sword.

Bella's shrill whinny broke the silence and echoed all around the small cave. Both girls clapped their hands over their ears.

No more than three seconds later, they heard an answering neigh and loud rhythm of galloping hooves on stone. Stephen jerked around, sword in front of him, and the girls and ponies were forgotten for the moment.

"Stephen! Stop! They are only children. Why don't you pick on someone your own size?" Ms. Cavalieri and Willow appeared in the cave, as if by magic. Ms. Cavalieri had a foil in her hand and was glittering in her armor. "What's wrong? Scared?"

Stephen laughed. "Erin. You know better than that but nice try. You need to join me. You are perfect for my team. You know you don't really care about these girls." The hawk flew from his arm and landed on a stone ledge above.

"You're wrong, Stephen. I won't let you harm them. And I won't ever join you." She stepped closer and out into the light as she said this, and she raised her delicate weapon. "Come on."

Stephen's face suddenly went from laughing to anger. Willow snorted and tried to move in front of Ms. Cavalieri.

"Willow, no. This is between us." Willow shook her head and stood her ground. Ms. Cavalieri put her hand on Willow's neck, and they seemed to have a second of understanding. Willow moved to the side but did not move back.

The two warriors moved closer to each other, everything forgotten but the other. Neither girl nor pony made a sound. They seemed to hardly even take a breath. Swords flicked back silently. Maggie closed her eyes.

Suddenly the whole cave exploded in noise! The sound of shouting and hooves overwhelmed Maggie's senses.

"Well, hello, old friend!" Bursting through the tunnel and into the cave was Darren McMillan, followed by the massive Coal. Sam and Lyndsey with Jazz and Reece and Athena were right behind him as well. "I was hoping we would get to spend some time together. Erin, move out of my way."

Ms. Cavalieri glared at Mr. McMillan but moved back, never taking her eyes off of Stephen. "Willow, get Bella and the girls." Ms. Cavalieri spoke so sharply that it startled Maggie. Willow pranced around Stephen cautiously and approached the small group of three. She walked up to Bella and touched noses with her, blowing soothingly into the smaller pony's nose. Then she struck out—squealing as she did—and broke the chain that held Bella as if it were made of straw.

Bella shook her head and nickered in relief as the chain fell to the ground with a loud *clank*.

"Maggie, get on your pony. Katie, hop on Willow." Ms. Cavalieri waved her sword at the other girls. "Mount up. Let's get out of here. Darren?"

"Go on, Erin, we have some unfinished business here." Darren and Stephen were circling each other, eyes never leaving one another. "I've been waiting for this day. Let's end this, once and for all."

The two men were almost exactly the same size. In fact, they had the same smirks on their faces, and it was almost impossible to tell who wanted this fight more.

"Ms. Cavalieri!" Sam shouted, "I hear more coming! We need to get out of here before we are trapped!" Lyndsey, Sam, and Reece were scrambling to get on their ponies.

Ms. Cavalieri hopped up behind Katie. "Darren, quit playing! Let's go! You can finish this later!"

The hawk on the ledge shifted slightly, making a soft cawing noise, but stayed in place at the sharp nod of Stephen's head.

Mr. McMillan stood his ground for a moment. Coal danced and snorted behind him, ears flicking back and tossing his thick forelock out of his eyes as the sound of hooves came closer. Mr. McMillan stuck his sword out toward Stephen. "This is your lucky day, brother." With that, he spun around and was on Coal in a heartbeat. "Up!" he shouted, and all the ponies and horses took a few leaps and were straining straight up toward the sunlight. Maggie closed her eyes as her stomach lurched. Suddenly she was warm and everything was bright! They made it!

"Whew!" She heard Katie sigh, and then Katie gave a sharp whistle. Moments later, Maggie heard a pony squeal in delight as Lily came up beside Willow, bucking through the air in excitement.

"Lily! You missed all the fun!" Katie shouted, and the pony snorted in frustration.

Darren circled around behind them, making sure they weren't being followed.

"They won't follow us today," said Ms. Cavalieri, "but Stephen will be back."

Coal tossed his head haughtily, and Mr. McMillan did the same. "We'll be waiting."

Together they made their way through the sky back toward Blackwatch Stables.

CHAPTER THIRTEEN

Home Again

W hen they returned to the barn, they all quietly took care of their ponies, rubbing and brushing them until they were cool and ready for their dinner. They all got warm mash that night, and Maggie made sure that Bella had extra hay and fresh water. She stood in the stall with her arms wrapped around her pony, wishing that she didn't have to leave. Bella gave a soft nicker as Maggie traced the heart-shaped marking on her pony's face and pulled the stall door closed for the night.

∪∪∪

Mr. McMillan and Coal said a cool good-bye and strolled off at a prancing walk toward the sunset. Ms. Cavalieri was so mad at Maggie and Katie that she could hardly even speak to them. She did manage to mention that they would be doing barn chores and not riding for a month. It was worth it though. It was worth knowing that Bella was back at Blackwatch safe and sound.

∪∪∪

Her dad pulled up to the barn just as the darkness covered the barn. "Hi, kiddo!" Jeff said as he stepped out of the car and gave her a big hug. "Did you have a good day? Anything special happen?"

Maggie smiled wearily at her father. "Just a normal day at the barn." She heard Katie giggling behind her and smiled to herself as she climbed into the car.

That night, Maggie lay in bed while her dad was downstairs watching his favorite TV show, totally ignorant to what had gone on that day. They had enjoyed the usual dinner of omelets—this time Greek omelets—and talked about what they might do the following weekend.

"Hey, Maggie," Jeff said as he wiped down the counter, "I was cleaning up the attic today and came across something you might like to see." He walked over to a long, narrow wooden box that was sitting on the counter. "This was your mom's. She had mentioned that she was into fencing when she was young, but I never knew that she actually had one of these." As he spoke, he opened the box and drew out a shiny silver foil. "I think she would have wanted you to have it," Jeff said, a little misty-eyed as he handed it to Maggie. "Now don't play with it, it's pointy. But if you want, I will sign you up for fencing lessons. What a combo…fencing and horseback riding. Your mother was so special."

"Yes. She was," Maggie said, as she took the weapon and thought about the empty rack on Ms. Cavalieri's office wall. "She was so special."

∪∪∪

As Maggie dozed off, something bothered her, something that she had almost forgotten in all the excitement. In the back of her sleeping mind, she saw a small cave of forgotten horses. The white mare. There was something about her that was vaguely familiar. In her dream, Maggie walked up to the mare and put her hand flat on her face. The horse looked into Maggie's eyes and a familiar voice whispered, "Maggie, this is Chloe." Maggie sat up with a start! *Mom!*

ABOUT THE AUTHOR

A mber Cavalier Spiler began her equestrian career at age five in the horse country of Ocala, Florida. Inspired and supported by her mother, Trish Cavalier, she began working with Mary Rivers, where she developed extensive knowledge that covered many breeds and styles of riding. Amber earned the title of National Champion Equitation Rider in the Paso Fino breed as well as four other national championships and several regional and state championships. Life took her away from horses for twenty years. As life allowed,

Amber rekindled her passion while watching her daughters, Bella and Lily, learn to ride and experience the excitement that had consumed her as a young girl. Then she found Toby, her current horse, through CANTER Mid-Atlantic (an organization that places thoroughbreds into good homes when their racing careers end). It is with this lifelong enthusiasm for horses that Amber decided to pen the *Blackwatch Stables* series, weaving her own experiences into this delightful story.

For more information about *The Secret of Blackwatch* and upcoming books in the *Blackwatch Stables* series, please visit:

www.blackwatchstablesseries.com.

Turn the page for a sneak peek into the second book in the *Blackwatch Stables* series...

BOOK TWO

BLACKWATCH STABLES

SNEAK PEEK

CHAPTER ONE

Sneak Peek

Maggie wiped the dirt from her face as she finished sweeping the aisle of the barn. She reached her hand into her pocket and pulled out a treat. She smiled as she heard the soft nicker from her pony.

Maggie slid the stall door open and held the treat out to Bella, who took it gently with her soft lips. When Bella finished the treat, she shoved Maggie with her head.

"Sorry, Bella," Maggie said out loud, "I still have one more week before I can ride again."

Bella snorted and shook her head. *Should have followed the rules*, thought Bella. *I would have been fine.*

Maggie rolled her eyes at her pony. Three weeks ago, Bella had been kidnapped, and Maggie, her best friend Katie, and Katie's sweet black pony Lily had broken the rules and gone off on their own to rescue Bella. Ms. Cavalieri, the barn owner and trainer, had been furious. She banned them from riding for a month. They also had to spend their days at the barn cleaning. Not just the usual pony brushing and tack care, but deep cleaning. Every corner and nook in the barn had been cleaned at least twice by one of the girls. The ponies were grouchy because they weren't being ridden.

"Maggie," Maggie turned to see Katie striding toward her, cobwebs in her hair, "are you finished?"

"Yep. I swept out every piece of hay in this place," said Maggie.

"Want to walk the ponies in the back field? Maybe we can hop up once we get out of sight and take a quick gallop?" Katie's eyes twinkled. She was fearless.

Maggie giggled as she heard Lily snort and kick the wall of the stall beside them. "I have a feeling Lily doesn't approve." Maggie smiled. "She doesn't want us in any more trouble."

"Chicken," taunted Katie, and just as she said that, Ms. Cavalieri walked up to the stall.

"Ladies, the barn looks nice. Why don't you take your ponies out to the back field and graze them by the lake?"

"Yes, Ms. Cavalieri," both girls said. Katie gave Maggie a little wink.

"Oh, and, girls, if I hear that you were on the ponies, you will be on probation for another month. That means that you will not have time to prepare for the first show of the season." With that, Ms. Cavalieri turned and marched away.

Maggie gave Katie that "I told you so" look, and Katie just glared at Maggie.

"I think she can read minds," said Katie, pouting as she pulled Lily's halter over the pony's black face.

Maggie laughed as she led Bella out of the stall and down the freshly swept aisle.

The girls were sprawled out in the plush grass, taking in the late spring warmth. Katie propped up on an elbow, looking at Maggie thoughtfully.

"Your birthday is coming up." Katie smiled. "Is there anything special that you want?"

Maggie sat up, crossing her legs and glancing at the grazing ponies. "I seriously can't think of a thing. I have a pony; what more could I want?" Maggie picked a long stem of grass and chewed on it thoughtfully. "I would like to go to a horse show this year. Something for the show would be great."

Katie nodded in agreement. "Great idea! This will only be my second show season."

"Do you think that I will like Eventing or Hunters?" asked Maggie as she watched Bella go from one patch of clover to another.

"Uh, Eventing, of course," smirked Katie. "It's way more fun!"

Maggie looked down. She had seen pictures of her mom dressed in her formal navy blue show coat, crisp white shirt with tan pants, and shiny black boots, sitting on an impeccably braided Chloe, and she had dreamed of looking the same.

The thought of galloping through an open field made her nervous though. *What if Bella tripped? Or fell over one of those solid jumps? What if a dragon came and got Bella again?* Maggie shuddered at the thought.

"Maggie? Maggie!" Katie was watching Maggie closely now. "Are you ready?"

"Yep," Maggie said as she planted a fake smile on her face and glanced quickly at the sky. "Let's head back."

Bella and Lily trotted toward the girls, and they all turned toward the barn and started walking back. The girls walked with their arms draped over the ponies' withers.

"You know you're safe. Right?" Katie looked at Maggie.

"Yeah, I know." Bella brushed her head against Maggie. It was a comforting gesture. "But one day we will have to all meet again. Soon."

The girls' and ponies' eyes met.

"Yeah, one day."

Maggie and Katie walked into the barn, ponies walking behind them, as the other girls were gathering around the door of the barn lounge.

"What's going on?" asked Katie.

"We have a new horse coming to Blackwatch Stables!" said Sam. "And rider!"

"Yay! I won't be the new girl anymore," said Maggie, smiling at the other girls.

"Oh yes you will," laughed Lyndsey. "He's a boy!"

All the girls giggled.

"I'm glad we finally have a boy—less giggling," said Sam, rolling her eyes at the other girls.

"You can say that again." The girls whipped around to see Ms. Cavalieri walking toward them. "He has no idea about your ponies. His pony is not magical, and you ladies must work hard to guard our secret." Now all the girls were staring at Ms. Cavalieri. "Don't look at me like I have three heads. We need some normal in this place. It keeps us all grounded and makes us more cautious. Quite frankly, this will make you all better riders." Ms. Cavalieri looked at each of them. "When we show, we can't cheat. We have to learn courses and tests on our own. Our ponies have to jump, not fly. As we work and ride around the new guy, we will become accustomed to acting like we have regular ponies."

The girls all started talking at once.

"His pony, Spot, comes in tomorrow," said Ms. Cavalieri over their chatter. "From what I've been told, he is super athletic and will give someone in this barn a run for their money in the Jumper ring." She glanced over at Sam, who crossed her arms and raised her eyebrows. "Girls, I would appreciate it if you and your ponies would go out of your way to make them feel at home." Ms. Cavalieri turned and started walking toward her office. "Oh, ladies, don't forget to tell him the rules." She smiled to herself as she walked into her office and closed the door.

The girls all stood around, looking at each other.

"Has this ever happened before?" asked Katie.

"Not that I know of," said Sam, looking to Lyndsey and Reece to see them shrugging as well.

Bella gave Maggie a shove with her head, reminding Maggie that they were standing in the middle of the barn, and she was getting hungry.

Maggie and Katie led their ponies back to their stalls, each one taking in the new information.

Wow. Stranger things certainly have happened. This is just part of being a student at Blackwatch Stables.